For Davis, Lila, Breck, and Grace—
I hope some of you make it.
—BM

For Mom, my first and
best art teacher.
—MW

Text © 2019 Brandon Mull
Illustrations © 2019 Michael Walton

Art direction by Richard Erickson
Design by Sheryl Dickert Smith

Visit us at shadowmountain.com

Library of Congress Cataloging-in-Publication Data

Names: Mull, Brandon, 1974– author. | Walton, Mike, 1975– illustrator.
Title: Smarter than a monster : a survival guide / written by Brandon Mull ; illustrated by Mike Walton.
Description: Salt Lake City, Utah : Shadow Mountain, [2019] | Summary: Learn how to defeat monsters by practicing good health habits, including brushing and flossing teeth, keeping a clean room, and being active instead of sitting in front of the television all afternoon.
Identifiers: LCCN 2019008877 | ISBN 9781629726106 (hardbound : alk. paper)
Subjects: | CYAC: Monsters—Fiction. | Cleanliness—Fiction. | Health—Fiction.
Classification: LCC PZ7.M9112 Sm 2019 | DDC [E]—dc23 LC record available at https://lccn.loc.gov/2019008877

Printed in China   4/2019
RR Donnelley, Dongguan, Guangdong, China

10   9   8   7   6   5   4   3   2   1

SMARTER THAN A MONSTER

A SURVIVAL GUIDE

Written by
BRANDON MULL

Illustrated by
MIKE WALTON

SHADOW
MOUNTAIN

Our imaginations have created monsters since the beginning of time. The only reason to fear monsters is if we give them power. The more you learn about monsters, the more you will know how to defeat them and keep them away. Just ask a librarian.

NO MONSTER WANTS YOU TO READ THIS BOOK.

The first place most kids expect to find a monster is in the closet. The second place is under the bed. These are common mistakes.

No self-respecting monster would hide in such obvious places.

If you happen to find a monster in the closet or under your bed, it will be a very pathetic creature.

If you order it to fetch you a snack, it will probably make you a peanut butter sandwich and pour you a glass of milk.

Certain fierce monsters have learned that frightened kids will sometimes sneak into bed with their parents, so these clever predators hide under the parents' bed where nobody thinks to check.

Usually, monsters leave kids alone when they are in their own beds, making your bed a fairly safe place.

Monsters like dirt and grime.

If a monster could choose between two kids,
it will usually eat the filthy one.

Taking regular baths is a good way to keep most monsters away. Not only do they avoid clean children, monsters hate the smell of soap.

Foul breath is like perfume to a monster. Kids who remember to brush and floss their teeth every night usually survive to be teenagers.

Monsters often strike when you are not paying attention. They use television and video games as bait, because kids are sitting still for a long time, staring in one direction. The more time you spend in front of the television, the greater your chances of becoming a monster snack.

One good way to keep monsters from launching a surprise attack against you is to keep your room clean. Monsters love to hide in a messy room. If there are toys and clothes all over the floor, you are in a perfect position to be ambushed by a monster.

Be careful whenever you see something that looks terribly out of place. For example, if you find a wonderful birthday cake sitting at the edge of a swamp, it is probably a monster trap. Same with a go-kart in a mortuary. Or a carousel in a ghost town.

Some kids are afraid of clowns. This is a natural instinct, because a lot of monsters look just like clowns. How can you tell a good clown from a bad one? Environment! If you see a clown at a circus or a party, you are probably safe. But if you meet a clown out in the woods, run for your life.

Dressing up like a monster is a good form of camouflage.
Monsters seldom bother other monsters. The safest day
of the year from a monster attack is Halloween, which
monsters think is a big parade in their honor.

Sometimes imagining an endless variety of monsters can be stressful. But your imagination is powerful enough that you can also imagine ways to outsmart and defeat them. Be smart, stay strong, and you'll never need to worry about monsters again.

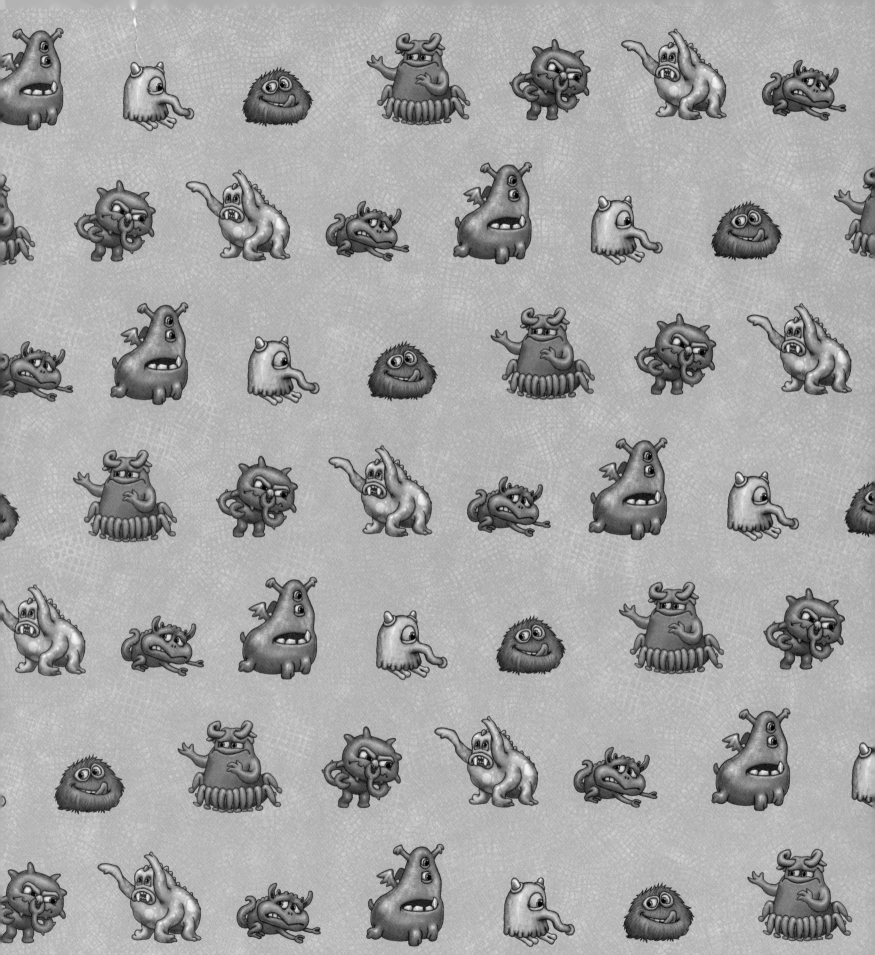